A Note to Parents and Caregivers:

Read-it! Readers are for children who are just starting on the amazing road to reading. These beautiful books support both the acquisition of reading skills and the love of books.

The RED LEVEL presents familiar topics using common words and repeating sentence patterns.
The BLUE LEVEL presents new ideas using a larger vocabulary and varied sentence structure.
The YELLOW LEVEL presents more challenging ideas, a broad vocabulary, and wide variety in sentence structure.

When sharing a book with your child, read in short stretches, pausing often to talk about the pictures. Have your child turn the pages and point to the pictures and familiar words. And be sure to reread favorite stories or parts of stories.

There is no right or wrong way to share books with children. Find time to read with your child, and pass on the legacy of literacy.

Adria F. Klein, Ph.D.
Professor Emeritus
California State University
San Bernardino, California

First American edition published in 2003 by
Picture Window Books
5115 Excelsior Boulevard
Suite 232
Minneapolis, MN 55416
1-877-845-8392
www.picturewindowbooks.com

First published in Great Britain by Franklin Watts, 96 Leonard Street, London, EC2A 4XD
Text © Maggie Moore 2001
Illustration © Rob Hefferan 2001

Printed in the United States of America.

Library of Congress Cataloging-in-Publication Data
Moore, Maggie.
  The three little pigs / by Maggie Moore ; illustrated by Rob Hefferan.—1st American ed.
    p. cm. — (Read-it! fairy tale readers)
  Summary: Tells the story of three little pigs who leave home to seek their fortunes and
how they deal with the big bad wolf.
  ISBN 1-4048-0071-9
  [1. Folklore. 2. Pigs—Folklore.] I. Hefferan, Rob, ill. II. Title. III. Series.
  PZ8.1.M7796 Th 2003
  398.24′529633—dc21
        [E]   2002072292

PICTURE WINDOW BOOKS
Minneapolis, Minnesota

The Three Little Pigs

Written by Maggie Moore

Illustrated by Rob Hefferan

Reading Advisors:
Adria F. Klein, Ph.D.
Professor Emeritus, California State University
San Bernardino, California

Ruth Thomas
Durham Public Schools
Durham, North Carolina

R. Ernice Bookout
Durham Public Schools
Durham, North Carolina

Todd Hall School
3925 W. Lunt
Lincolnwood, IL 60712

Picture Window Books
Minneapolis, Minnesota

Once upon a time, there were three little pigs.

5

One day, the three little pigs decided to leave home.

"Watch out for the big, bad wolf," said their mother as she waved good-bye.

The first little pig built a
house of straw.

The second little pig built
a house of sticks.

The third little pig built a
house of bricks.

A big, bad wolf sneaked up
to the house of straw.

"Let me in, little pig, let me in," he growled.

"Not by the hairs on my chinny chin chin," said the first little pig.

"Then I'll huff and I'll puff and I'll blow your house in!" cried the big, bad wolf.

So, he huffed and he puffed
and he blew the house in.

Then the wolf sneaked up
to the house of sticks.

"Let me in, little pig, let me in," he growled.

"Not by the hairs on my chinny chin chin," said the second little pig.

"Then I'll huff and I'll puff and I'll blow your house in!" cried the big, bad wolf.

So, he huffed and he puffed
and he blew the house in.

Then the wolf sneaked up
to the house of bricks.

"Let me in, little pig, let me in," he growled.

"Not by the hairs on my chinny chin chin," said the third little pig.

"Then I'll huff and I'll puff
and I'll blow your house in!"
cried the big, bad wolf.

And he huffed and he puffed and he HUFFED and he PUFFED—

but he couldn't blow the
house of bricks in.

The wolf was VERY angry.
He climbed onto the roof.

"I'm coming to get you!"
he shouted down the
chimney to the little pigs.

The third little pig quickly put a pot of boiling water underneath the chimney.

The wolf fell down the chimney, right into the pot of boiling water.

And the three little pigs lived happily ever after in their house of bricks.

Red Level

The Best Snowman, by Margaret Nash 1-4048-0048-4
Bill's Baggy Pants, by Susan Gates 1-4048-0050-6
Cleo and Leo, by Anne Cassidy 1-4048-0049-2
Felix on the Move, by Maeve Friel 1-4048-0055-7
Jasper and Jess, by Anne Cassidy 1-4048-0061-1
The Lazy Scarecrow, by Jillian Powell 1-4048-0062-X
Little Joe's Big Race, by Andy Blackford 1-4048-0063-8
The Little Star, by Deborah Nash 1-4048-0065-4
The Naughty Puppy, by Jillian Powell 1-4048-0067-0
Selfish Sophie, by Damian Kelleher 1-4048-0069-7

Blue Level

The Bossy Rooster, by Margaret Nash 1-4048-0051-4
Jack's Party, by Ann Bryant 1-4048-0060-3
Little Red Riding Hood, by Maggie Moore 1-4048-0064-6
Recycled!, by Jillian Powell 1-4048-0068-9
The Sassy Monkey, by Anne Cassidy 1-4048-0058-1
The Three Little Pigs, by Maggie Moore 1-4048-0071-9

Yellow Level

Cinderella, by Barrie Wade 1-4048-0052-2
The Crying Princess, by Anne Cassidy 1-4048-0053-0
Eight Enormous Elephants, by Penny Dolan 1-4048-0054-9
Freddie's Fears, by Hilary Robinson 1-4048-0056-5
Goldilocks and the Three Bears, by Barrie Wade 1-4048-0057-3
Mary and the Fairy, by Penny Dolan 1-4048-0066-2
Jack and the Beanstalk, by Maggie Moore 1-4048-0059-X
The Three Billy Goats Gruff, by Barrie Wade 1-4048-0070-0